CITY SLICKER

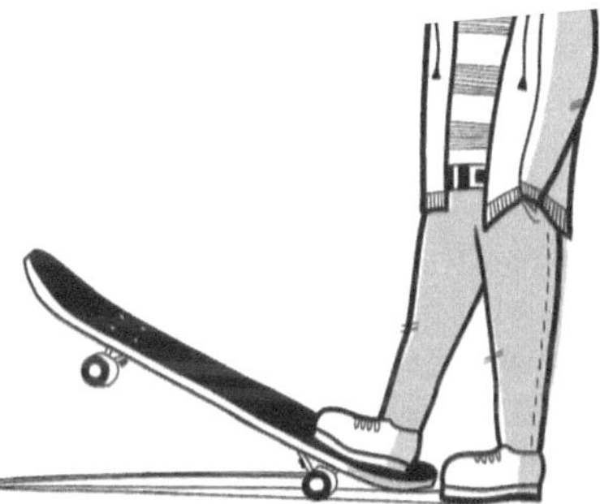

PHIL KETTLE & BOB ANDERSEN

Illustrated by Shane McGowan

First published in Australia in 2019 by
 Wellington (Aust) Pty Ltd
(ACN062 365 413)
433 Wellington Street
Clifton Hill, Vic. 3068
Australia

A catalogue record for this
book is available from the
National Library of Australia

City Slicker
ISBN: 978-1-925308-37-2

Designed by Workingtype Pty Ltd
Printed in Australia by IngramSpark

Contents

Welcome to the Outback

Three months ago, my life changed in a way that I never dreamed possible. It was a Friday and it was the thirteenth day of the month, which is supposed to be unlucky for some. And that Friday was definitely unlucky for my Uncle Buck.

Uncle Buck owned a HUGE sheep station way out woop-woop, and he had been mustering sheep all day when a wild storm struck. Sadly for Uncle Buck, he was hit by lightning and sizzled like a sausage on a very hot barbecue.

When we received the news, Mum and Dad were VERY, VERY sad, but that all changed a few weeks later when we got an unexpected call from Uncle Buck's lawyer. It turns out that Uncle Buck had left his sheep station to my family in his will. Mum and Dad's tears turned to smiles – suddenly we owned a sheep station in outback Australia!

Two days later, we had a family meeting to decide what we were going to do. It was decided by two votes to one that we were leaving our city home and moving to the outback. (You can probably guess who was the 'one'.)

Faster than I could wave goodbye to my city friends, Mum and Dad packed up and headed off to Overflow Station, dragging me along with them.

My name is Clancy, I'm eleven years old and these are the stories of my outback adventures.

Meet the Gang

That's my mum...

and that's my dad.

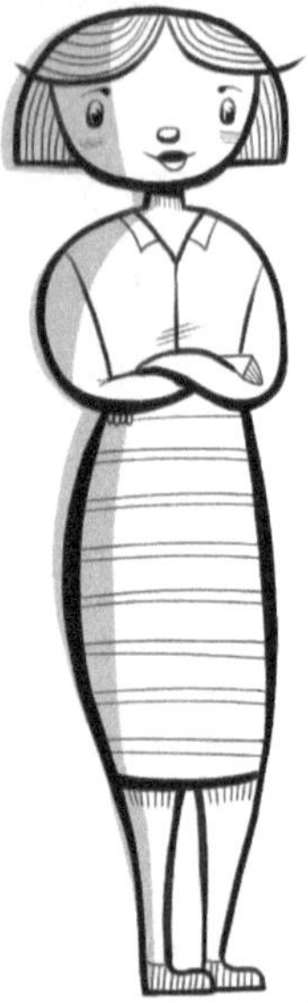

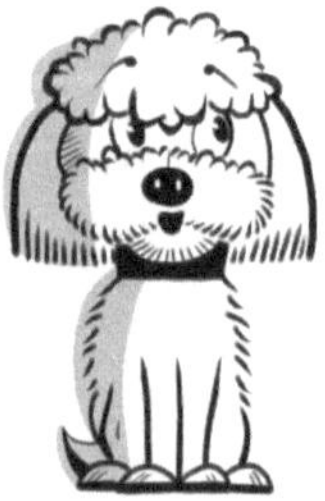

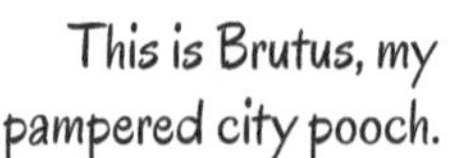

This is Brutus, my pampered city pooch.

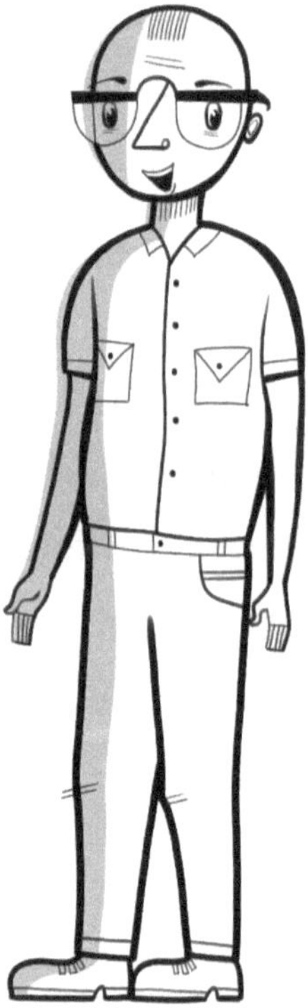

Big Bill is the
manager at Overflow
Station...

And that's Butters,
Little Bill's farm dog.

... and Little Bill
is his daughter!

Chapter 1
So This Is It?

Two days and 1200 kilometres after we left the city, we arrived way out woopwoop at our new outback home, Overflow Station, about 1000 hectares of not much of anything as far as I could tell. Not one single town, not a tram, train or bus to be seen. Although we did pass a big river at some point, the Darling River, Dad said. Big deal!

My first thought as I got out of our car was how the heck am I going to live here? And my second thought was how am I going to stay in touch with my friends? Then just as I was thinking that things couldn't possibly get worse, they did ... a lot worse. There was a girl waiting to greet us. Yep, that's right.

A GIRL!

'Hi,' said the girl. 'My name's Little Bill. My dad's Big Bill, the Overflow Station Manager. He sent me over here to say hello. I'm guessing you must be Clancy, the city kid?'

'Yes, I'm Clancy and I'm the city kid,' I said, rolling my eyes. 'My mum and dad told me there was another kid living here, but I thought that with a name like Little Bill, you'd be a boy.'

'Well, I'm not a boy,' announced Little Bill. 'And I wouldn't want to be, because most boys I know are pretty useless ... especially boys from the city.'

At that moment, I wanted to strangle Mum and Dad. I wanted to tell them to get right back in the car and drive back to the city NOW. I was wondering what I'd done that was so bad I was being made to live out here in the middle of nowhere as my punishment.

In my mind, I made a silent promise to whoever you make silent promises to that if I could just go back and live in the city – please, please, please, please, please – I'd be the best, most well-behaved and perfect boy ever. And I mean EVER!

'So, city boy,' Little Bill continued, 'now that you're living here in the outback, I'm here to help turn you into a country boy.'

'Yeah, well good luck with that, country girl,' I chuckled.

My dog, Brutus, had jumped out of the car and was sitting at my feet. She looked as miserable as I was feeling.

'What sort of dog is that?' asked Little Bill.

'A city dog,' I smiled.

'You mean not much good for anything?' said Little Bill.

Things just keep getting better and better, I thought.

'Well, I'll have to turn her into a country dog then,' said Little Bill, without so much as a smile crossing her face. 'Like our dogs. It'll take time, I guess. But if you listen to me, and watch everything I do, you'll fit right into country life in no time at all, and you'll probably be able to survive in the outback too.'

'And if I don't?' I asked.

'If you don't what?' she said.

'If I don't listen to you, and watch everything you do, then ... what?'

Little Bill narrowed her eyes and stared hard at me. 'What's the opposite of "survive"?' she asked.

I knew the answer to that, so I said nothing, walked around to the other side of the car and grabbed my backpack. Out of the corner of my eye, I saw Little Bill shrug her shoulders and walk off towards our gate.

Later on, Mum and Dad told me how lucky I was that I had Little Bill to show me the ropes. What ropes? I thought. But then I realised that showing me the ropes was like showing me around the place, sort of teaching me how to live the outback life.

I shut my eyes and groaned. This was not going to be fun.

Chapter 2
The First Morning

The next morning I was lying in my bed dreaming of home. I was thinking about trains, trams, cinemas, shopping malls, video games and take-away food. It was a really good dream. Until it turned into a nightmare.

'Get out of bed, city slicker! There's no sleeping in when you live out here. Time to rise and shine, there's things to do and things to see.'

What?! I rubbed my eyes. Was I still dreaming? Then I saw a shadowy figure standing at the end of my bed. And now I was sure I was having a nightmare, a country nightmare, and her name was Little Bill.

'This is the first and last time I'm going to tell you to get out of bed. If I have to come in again I'm going to throw a bucket of water over you!'

She turned and walked out of my room.

'It's still dark outside,' I said as I rolled back under the covers. How did she get into my room anyway?

'Well, the work day here starts before the sun rises,' I heard her call from down the hallway.

'MY day starts when I wake up,' I said to no one in particular.

I went back to sleep. I love sleeping in. Sleeping in is my favourite thing to do ... well, that and take-away food and video games.

Ten minutes after going back to sleep I was dreaming again, but this time I dreamt

that I was in the middle of a lake and about to drown!

'I told you that if I had to come back in here, I would throw a bucket of water over you, and might I add you're lucky that I didn't throw the bucket at you as well,' said Little Bill, who was now standing at the end of my bed with her hands on her hips.

If this is what life in the outback is going to be like, can someone please take me back to the city? I thought, as I dragged my half-drowned body out of bed. Note to self:

'Now,' said Little Bill, 'when you live in the outback, you've got to dress the right way. Those thongs that you were wearing on your feet yesterday have got to go in the bin, along with that stupid cap you had on your head. I've got you some boots and a proper hat, and from now on you'll wear jeans,' she finished.

Note to self:

In the end, I decided it was no good arguing with Little Bill. I think I knew already that there was no way I could win. I got into my new clothes, pulled on my new boots and grabbed my new hat, ready for whatever the day might bring.

Chapter 3
Little Bill's House

It turned out that Little Bill had already told Mum that I was going to her place before breakfast. And Mum said that was OK – thanks a lot, Mum!

The sun was still coming up as we shut our front door and walked over to the Station Manager's place, where Little Bill lived with her dad, Big Bill. Actually, I think that might have been the first sunrise that I have ever seen, and it wasn't so bad. Lots of pink and orange sky and fresh air as well. It wasn't such a bad start to the day – except for the bucket of water in bed, of course.

Little Bill's house was quite different from Uncle Buck's house. Uncle Buck's was on a hill but Little Bill's was up on poles – you had to climb up a flight of steps to get to the front door.

'Why the poles?' I asked.

'Because it floods here about two or three times a year,' said Little Bill. 'We don't like sleeping in the water.' She laughed to let me know she was joking. 'But it's quite exciting,' she continued. 'My dad has a tinny in the shed and if it looks like rain then he gets it out so that if anything serious happens we can choof off out of here. And take off your boots!'

We'd got to the front door.

We went inside – it was very dark and it took a while for my eyes to adjust.

'What's a tinny?' I asked. Little Bill looked at me as if I didn't have a clue. 'Do you know anything? she said. 'I'll take you to the shed in a minute and you can work it out for yourself.'

'Why doesn't Uncle Buck's house have poles?' I ask again.

Little Bill had the answer this time. 'Because Uncle Buck's is the big house and they had the sense to build on a hill so it doesn't get flooded. Our house is the manager's house and so it's on the river flat. Sometimes it floods even when it isn't even raining here.'

'How come?' I ask.

Little Bill is starting to get sick of all my questions. 'Because it's raining upstream in Queensland and so it floods here.'

The more I thought about it the more differences I saw. Uncle Buck's, or our house now, had a big veranda going all around the house but Little Bill's house had no veranda. Our house had five bedrooms but Little Bill's only had two.

It didn't take long to have a look around
the house so we put our boots back on
and went out to look at the tinny. There
in the shed was an aluminium dinghy
about 4 metres long with a big outboard
on the back. There was a boat trailer and,
on a rack on the wall, fishing rods, yabby

nets and special pots for … 'Murray River Crayfish,' said Little Bill.

'We used to go craying but they are endangered now and so we don't use the pots anymore. Also, some people don't like you using the yabby nets either. It's a conservation issue.'

By the tone of her voice, I wasn't at all sure whether Little Bill believed in conservation. In the city we all believe in conservation!

'If there is a flood we get in the boat and choof into town for supplies. I'll make sure we pick you up on the way through if you like.'

Wouldn't it be good to be surrounded by flood water? I thought. 'We wouldn't have to go to school! It'd be fun!' I said.

'Yep,' said Little Bill, 'but it gets pretty boring after a couple of days. You could try fishing off your veranda. Do you have a fishing rod?'

'I thought you said the water didn't come near our house?' I said.

Little Bill just shrugged. I think she felt she'd shown me enough for one day. 'Come back tomorrow and meet my dad,' she said.

Chapter 4
Meet Big Bill

The next morning Little Bill turned up really early to take me to her place for breakfast. She came in a battered old ute and she was actually driving it!

'How come you can drive?' I asked her as she climbed out from behind the steering wheel.

'I've been driving since I was six. That's what you get to do when you live on a property like this,' she explained. Then she told me to climb onto the passenger seat next to her. 'I can also ride a motor bike, a horse and practically anything else that moves.'

Brutus had followed me over to the ute as it pulled up.

'Get her in the back,' said Little Bill.

I leant down to lift Brutus up.

'What are you doing?' shouted Little Bill. 'If a dog can't jump into the back of a ute then it's not much of a dog! Get her to jump in!'

'Jump up, Brutus!' I cried. Brutus did nothing. 'She's not going to jump,' I said.

Little Bill muttered something about being overweight but I don't think Brutus is overweight. Plump, yes, but not overweight. I think Little Bill thinks I'm a bit out of condition too, but I'm already a lot thinner than I was in the city and I've only been here two days. I guess I've just been too busy to eat.

'Then we'll drive off and leave her. She'll soon learn to jump!' she said. She's a 'take-no-prisoners' sort of girl. Not sure what that means, but it was what Dad said last night when I asked him why he had let Little Bill wake me up that morning.

She started walking around to the front of the ute and so I lifted Brutus onto the tray. I don't think she noticed.

'The key to living out here,' said Little Bill in a way that told me she was serious, 'is to listen carefully.'

'To you!' I laughed. I was thinking I'd never get a chance to say anything.

Again I got one of those looks. 'No, listen to nature, you idiot! You come out here and if there's silence for a moment you feel you've got to fill it with your own voice. Yap, yap, yap! You make a big statement even though you don't have a clue what you're talking about. Or you complain – I feel like fried chicken, where can I get fish and chips, where's the soft drink? It drives me crazy! It would suit me if you just shut up and left it to me to do the talking.'

I felt bad then. Surely she could understand that I missed a lot of city things, and the food was a big one of them.

Big Bill, the Station Manager, was standing at the front door when we arrived. I definitely knew then why he was called Big Bill. His shoulders filled up the door frame, and his head almost touched the top of the door. I think he was the biggest man I'd ever seen!

'Hello, young fellow, welcome to Overflow Station,' he said as he put his hand out to shake mine. My hand totally disappeared in his and when he shook it I felt like my whole body was bouncing up and down.

'Son, your Uncle Buck built this property up from scratch with his own bare hands and hard work. Now it's one of the best sheep stations in Australia,' he said. 'He has left it to your family. I hope you treat it the way he would have wanted you to treat it.'

If I had my way we would sell it and move back to the city, I was thinking. But I didn't say anything.

'Now come in and eat. There's a lot that Little Bill wants to show and teach you.' He smiled as he ushered me inside.

Brutus hadn't left my side since I lifted her out of the back of the ute. She started

to walk inside with me. Big Bill stopped and looked down at her.

'So, what do you call that?' he asked, looking down at Brutus, who started to tremble and whimper.

'This is my dog, Brutus,' I said.

'It looks more like a toy than a dog,' laughed Big Bill. 'What does your dog do?'

'Well, she follows me around and she can fetch a ball,' I said.

'Hmmm, see over there,' said Big Bill, pointing towards a window.

'See what over where?' I asked.

'That tree in the paddock, over there.'

'Oh yes, I see it now,' I said.

'Well, that paddock is called the one-tree paddock, because as you can see there is only one tree in it. And under that tree lie many dogs that weren't able to do anything useful,' said Big Bill.

'But, I can't see any dogs,' I said.

'That, my little city-slicker friend, is

because they are lying below the ground,' Big Bill laughed.

Brutus whimpered again and moved quite a bit closer to me.

'Does Little Bill have a dog?' I asked Big Bill.

Note to self:

'Yep,' he said. 'It's outside, where dogs belong, and it's a real dog.' He said the word 'real' with emphasis.

'What's its name?' I asked

Big Bill looked a little disconcerted,

maybe even embarrassed. 'Butters,' he muttered.

'Boy or girl?' I asked

'Boy,' muttered Big Bill. 'Stupid name if you ask me.'

I didn't want to discuss the matter any further but I was pleased Little Bill had a dog and that it was a male dog. In my imagination I could see a real friendship developing between my Brutus and her Butters. I could see them rolling around in the grass together, chasing a ball together and generally having fun. Maybe they would have puppies together!

I was about to ask Big Bill about puppies but he looked so grumpy I decided against it. I decided to wait until I saw Butters in the flesh.

I guess you want to know how I got Brutus. It was in the Lost Dogs' Home. I'd been pestering Mum and Dad for a dog fora long time and eventually we all went down to the Dogs' Home and there she was. The girl at the Dog's Home said she was a Poodle-Bichon-Frise cross, meaning, Mum said, that the father was most probably a Poodle and the mother a Bichon-Frise.

The girl seemed to know a lot about dogs. 'This breed is from the Toy Dog group,' she said. Dad was incensed.

'Toy Dog group!' he cried. 'No son of mine is going to have a toy dog, however much it's alive!'

'It's OK, Dad,' I said, 'I'll call her Brutus so everyone will think she's a dangerous dog. If a burglar comes into the house we can just call out, 'Sic 'em, Brutus,' and the burglar will get such a fright he'll skedaddle.' This calmed Dad down a bit.

'Well, she's had her inoculations and so she's ready to go,' said the girl, who wasn't very impressed by Dad's yelling. 'You'd better get going,' she said, looking at Mum and me and avoiding Dad's steely glare. She handed me the little fluffy ball and said, 'Here you go, Brutus, Clancy is your new dad.'

I felt warm inside – in fact it was the best feeling I'd ever had.

'Where did you find Butters?' I asked Little Bill. I was still feeling a warm glow remembering how good I felt when I took Brutus home.

'You don't "find" a dog,' she said. 'That's ridiculous! The farm dogs here have puppies and when my dad spots a good puppy then he lets me know. The last time there were puppies the stronger ones were needed to work on the farm but Dad said I could have the runt of the litter – there's always one. I called him Butters because when he was small he used to like a piece

of toast with butter on it. He still likes it.
Do you want me to show you?'

She got a slice of bread out of the
cupboard and stuck it in the toaster.
Butters' nose was pushing against the
screen door – he could smell the toast
cooking. He was a huge dog!

'He's a really smart dog,' said Little Bill,
as we went outside onto the veranda. She

gave Butters a tickle under his ear. 'Not like that fluffball you found!'

That warm feeling I had suddenly drained away.

Little Bill went back inside when she heard the toast fly out of the toaster. She buttered it and brought it outside again and then woof! It was gone. Butters looked expectantly for more.

'No, that's it!' she said firmly. She was one tough hombre!

We went through to the kitchen.

'Lamb chops and fried eggs, the perfect breakfast for hard-working country people,' Big Bill announced as we sat down to a very full table. There was a plate of sizzling lamb chops, and another of fried eggs, and about a whole loaf of toasted bread. In fact, there was so much food, I didn't know how I was going to eat it all, but I was pretty sure I would give it a good try.

'Wow, I didn't think we would eat lamb chops out here,' I said after a while, when I was starting to feel really full.

'Why on earth not?' asked Big Bill. He seemed slightly amused by my question.

'Well, in the city lamb chops come from a supermarket,' I explained. 'And I haven't seen any supermarkets out here. In fact, I haven't seen any shops at all!'

Little Bill started to laugh. She laughed so hard that she very nearly fell off her chair. I didn't really see what was so funny.

'Clancy, you have so much to learn,' she said finally, wiping the tears from her eyes. 'Where do you think lamb chops come from before they get to the shop?'

'Well, they certainly don't grow on a lamb-chop tree,' I said.

'Look out there and tell me what you see,' said Little Bill, pointing out beyond one-tree paddock.

'I can see sheep,' I said.

'Well, that's where lamb chops come from,' Little Bill laughed again. 'Right here on the station.'

'Next time we need to get lamb chops, you can come with me and I'll show you how it's done,' Big Bill added.

Brutus whimpered again. Now that's something I'm definitely going to try and avoid doing, I thought to myself.

Breakfast was soon finished. And I have to admit, the lamb chops didn't taste anywhere near as good as the ones that my mum got from the shops in the city – they tasted way better!

'You've got to be tough to survive out here in the outback,' Little Bill said as I collected up the plates and the cutlery. 'Just look at you, soft hands like they've never done a day's work! You look like a real city slicker.'

'Well, maybe that's because I am a real

city slicker,' I said. 'And there's nothing wrong with that.'

'Not if you live in the city,' Little Bill replied. 'But you're in the outback now.'

'That's right,' said Big Bill. 'Your Uncle Buck would want us to toughen you up, just like he would have done if he was here. It's our duty.'

Hmmm, if Uncle Buck hadn't been sizzled like a sausage on a barbecue when he was hit by lightning, I'd still be back in the city where I belong, I thought. But I didn't say it.

'Well, today is going to be the first day of your outback education,' Little Bill continued.

'Gee, aren't I lucky?' I said. 'At least I must look like I belong in the outback with these boots, check shirt, jeans and cowboy hat.'

Little Bill just laughed. 'My teacher tells

me that you should never judge a book by its cover,' she explained, 'but you are the least likely person I've ever seen to belong in the outback. Even in your new clothes.'

Little Bill was probably right, considering the closest I had ever been to the outback before was probably the park back in my street in the city. Then Little Bill informed me that she'd actually been to the city twice, and on both occasions she couldn't wait to leave. I didn't bother arguing with that. The city was probably a lot safer for the rest of us when she did go back to the outback. I just shrugged my shoulders. Even if Overflow Station wasn't where I wanted to be, I had no choice but to grin and bear it. So I told her that we may as well get on with our day.

Chapter 5
Listen and Learn

'Don't ask any questions, just listen and learn,' Little Bill said as we walked out 'the door of her house. I just quietly rolled my eyes.

'The Overflow is one of the biggest stations in New South Wales,' she went on. 'The property is cut down the middle by the Darling River, and without that river, nothing on this station would survive.'

That made me chuckle. 'Well, I might be from the city,' I said, 'but even I know that you have to have water. How else could you shower, water the garden and boil eggs?'

'Hey, I told you to listen and learn,' said

Little Bill. 'No questions, remember?' Boy, this girl was annoying, I thought. But I had nothing better to do, so I followed her over to the ute.

I have to admit, I was just a little bit impressed at how she drove off, even though she had to sit on a cushion to see over the steering wheel. I can't drive, although I was pretty good on my scooter and my bike back in the city.

Then I remembered the horse outside the supermarket where my mum used to do the shopping. That was a plastic horse with a slot in its head where you had to put a dollar to make it go. I told Little Bill that I felt that I probably would be able to ride a horse because when I rode that one in the shop, I never fell off. Little Bill just laughed and told me I had an awful lot to learn.

Then we drove past the shearing sheds where shearing takes place once a year.

I told Little Bill that a sheep shearer was like a hairdresser for sheep and she laughed again. In fact, every time I told her something she seemed to laugh. Either she thought that I was very stupid or VERY FUNNY!

We saw kangaroos, lots of kangaroos, big and small, joeys too. I've never seen so many kangaroos! Now even though I was from the city, I knew that a lot of kangaroos together is called a 'mob' and this had to be the biggest mob I'd ever seen! Little Bill just kept on driving across the paddock, dodging this way and that, as they jumped alongside us or occasionally crossed the track in front of us. They didn't seem to bother her at all, and she didn't really seem to bother them either.

Then we saw a whole flock of huge birds – emus! They couldn't fly, but they could run really fast – especially away from the

ute. (And I didn't blame them, given how fast Little Bill was driving.) There were big ones and small ones too. Later, Little Bill explained to me that in emu families, the males look after the chicks. She said that was a bit like her dad and her.

Suddenly I felt the need to do what I always feel the need to do when I've been in a car for way too long ... PEE! I didn't really know how to tell Little Bill, so I shifted around in my seat for a little while, but eventually I knew I'd have to say something.

'Er, this is a bit embarrassing, but can you take me to the nearest toilet?' I said to Little Bill.

Lucky for me, Little Bill stopped the ute immediately.

'Thanks,' I said. 'But I can't see a toilet?'

'See that tree over there,' she said, pointing to a single gum tree in the distance.

'Yes,' I said.

'Well, that's a PEE tree,' she replied.

'But it just looks like every other tree out here, and I can't see a sign that says that it's a pee tree,' I said.

'Just go,' Little Bill laughed, 'before it's too late!'

Well, now I know that when you live in the outback, and you've got to go, you just go, and it doesn't really seem to matter where you go. It was only my second day out here and already I was starting to understand that living in the outback is totally different from living in the city!

Chapter 6
Listen Harder and Learn More

Suddenly, Little Bill stopped the ute in the middle of the bush and turned the engine off. 'Hey, tell me what you can hear?' she said.

'The only thing I can hear is you talking,' I said back.

'Hey, do all city people think they're smart like you think you're smart?' Little Bill asked.

And when I looked at her face, what I did know was that I was smart enough to know I'd better not say anything!

'What you are hearing is the sounds of the great outback,' she smiled.

'But the only sounds I can hear are birds singing and a breeze rustling the grass and the leaves in the trees,' I said.

'Well, that's the sounds of the great outback!' she laughed.

'That's pretty boring, if you ask me; no train, tram, bus or car noises,' I protested.

Little Bill just gave me one of those 'what's-wrong-with-you' looks. She was pretty good at them, actually.

'So, Clancy, do you think you can drive a vehicle or would that be too hard for a city slicker like you?' Little Bill asked, and jumped out of her side of the ute.

Now that was a challenge that was way too tempting to resist.

'If you can drive, I can too,' I replied, and I jumped out of my side of the ute almost as fast as she did.

'Well, we'll see about that,' she laughed.

Before I had time to say that actually,

I had never driven anything before –
although my teacher back in the city had
said more than once that I drove her crazy
– I was behind the steering wheel.

'So, come on then, away you go,' said Little
Bill. She didn't sound very encouraging. In
fact, she sounded quite amused.

'I'm not used to utes,' I said. 'What do I
do now?'

'Turn the ignition key and that will start the motor,' she smiled.

'Then what?'

'Push the clutch in – that's the pedal on the left – and put the ute in gear,' she said.

OK, so I got that far, then I paused.

'Now put your foot on the accelerator – that's the pedal on the right – and at the same time, take your foot off the clutch.'

I did exactly as she said. How hard could driving really be? The ute took off – fast!

'Now what do I do?' I yelled over the noise of the engine.

'Take your foot off the accelerator and put the same foot on the brake – that's the pedal in between the accelerator and the clutch,' Little Bill yelled back.

I did as I was told. I lifted my foot from the accelerator and slammed it down again.

REALLY HARD!

CRASH! BANG! CRASH!

'Are you okay?' I asked.

The ute had stopped, but the engine was still running.

'I'm OK, are you OK?' Little Bill asked. She was trying to stop laughing.

'What's so funny about driving into a tree?' I asked, as if I didn't know. But I thought she should probably take the fact that we'd just had a car accident at least a little bit seriously.

'You put your foot back on the accelerator instead of the brake,' she said, still laughing. 'That was hilarious!'

'So, what do we do now?' I said. 'If you could stop laughing for just a minute.'

'I guess we do what other great outback adventurers do,' Little Bill replied. 'Turn off the engine, because I don't think the ute is going anywhere else today. Lucky for us, this is a shady tree that you drove into. So we'll just sit here under it and hope that someone

comes along and saves us,' she finished.

'And what if they don't?' I said. I did not want to spend the night in the ute with Little Bill.

'Well, then we just die, dry up, turn to dust and blow away,' she winked.

'You can't be serious,' I said. 'We could be here all night!'

'You're probably right,' she continued. 'I guess the other option is that we can walk home.'

'And how far is that?' I asked.

'I reckon about seven kilometres,' said Little Bill. 'We've got water bottles. It will take most of the day, but we should be ok.'

'And how do we know which way to go?' I asked.

'We throw a stick up in the air and whichever way the skinny end points when it lands, we'll go in that direction,' she said.

I just rolled my eyes. I wanted to die.

OK, maybe I didn't want to die. But I really wanted to get back to the city right now.

'Hey, city slicker,' Little Bill winked. 'I'm only joking. I know the way home,' she said, pointing towards the river. 'All we have to do is walk that way for about a kilometre, and then all we need to do is follow the river and we will be home before dinner.'

I figured I didn't really have much choice but to follow her.

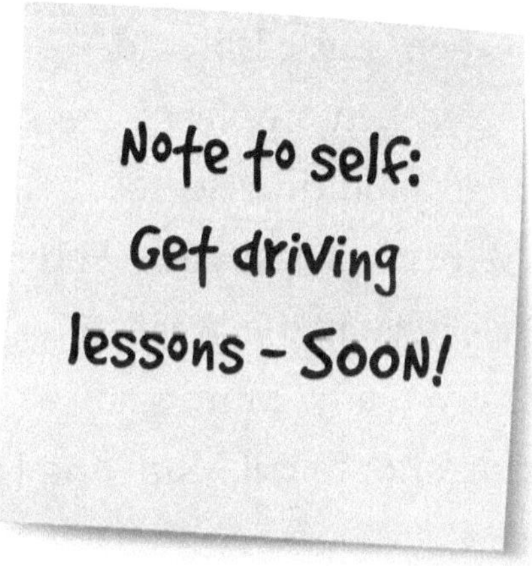

Chapter 7
A Big Day

After three hours of walking and three hours of being told how much I had to learn and how hard it was going to be to teach me, we arrived back at the homestead just as the sun was starting to set.

'Tomorrow we're going horse riding. Make sure you're up and dressed at dawn. See you then,' Little Bill said.

My legs ached, my feet were sore and I was hungry and thirsty.

'You've been gone all day! You and Little Bill must have had a great time. Go wash up, dinner's ready,' Mum said.

I decided not to tell Mum and Dad what happened.

'Let's just say that it has been a day that I will never forget,' I said. 'What's for dinner?'

'Lamb chops,' Mum said.

'Oh good, just what I was hoping for.'

I went to bed early after my second full day on Overflow Station. I knew that Little Bill would be waking me up in the morning if I slept in.

I had the strangest dreams. I dreamt I was a racing-car driver and I kept crashing. Then I realised it wasn't a dream, it was a nightmare!

Outback Jokes

What do you call a bunch of sheep
standing in a row?
A baa-baa queue.

What do you get from a nervous cow?
Milkshakes.

Why did the ram run over the cliff?
He didn't see the ewe turn!

Why did the emu cross the road?
To prove he wasn't a chicken.

Why did the wallaby cross the road?
Because it was the chicken's day off.

Why did the dingo cross the road?
To be just like the emu.

Why did the dingo cross the road twice?
Because he was double-crossed.

Why did the cockatoo sit on the clock?
Because he wanted to be on time.

Outback Facts

The Darling River

The Darling River is part of the MurrayDarling river system, one of the largest river systems in the world. It measures 1472 kilometres from its source in northern New South Wales to Wentworth, in southern New South Wales, where it joins the Murray River.

Including all its tributaries, the Darling River covers 2844 kilometres, making it the longest river system in Australia.

Today, people from about forty different indigenous groups live along the MurrayDarling basin, caring for country around the rivers, creeks, lakes and billabongs. Records show that indigenous people have been living in this area for about 30,000 years.

The rivers and their floodplains provided food, water, medicines, shelter, transport and fire. About 40 different groups lived in different parts of the river basin. The largest group was, and still is, the Barkindji. The Aboriginal name for the Darling River is Barka – Barkindji means the people of the Barka.

In 1828, the explorer Charles Sturt was sent by the Governor of New South Wales, Sir Ralph Darling, to find the path of the

Macquarie River. As a result, he arrived at the Darling River in 1829, and named it after the Governor.

European settlement brought change. Huge sheep and cattle stations were established and by the late 1830s, many indigenous people had lost access to waterways, land and sacred sites. Hostile confrontations between settlers and indigenous people occurred.

Between the 1850s and the 1890s, the government created more than twenty indigenous 'reserves' in the area. This marked the end of 'shared' occupation and the beginning of severe restrictions on indigenous people's access to the land.

In 1859, the first paddle steamer, the *Albury*, headed off up the Darling, delivering cargo to Mt Murchison Station and returning with 100 bales of wool. By 1865, paddle steamers were carrying both wool and copper down the Darling. The wool industry was the backbone of the river trade. With new and more powerful steamers, and longer and wider barges, the volume of wool transported by paddle steamer increased rapidly.

But river conditions were unpredictable. Farmers and shipping companies learnt to work around the high and low water levels in the Darling. During one huge flood, a paddle steamer paddled all the way up the Paroo River to the Queensland border, almost 300 kilometres from the Darling River. On the other hand, the *Jane Eliza* holds the record for the longest time a boat was stranded in the Darling River during dry conditions – three whole years.

In 1880, when roads and railways were built, many parts of outback New South Wales became accessible by land. This marked the beginning of the end for paddle steamers and river trade. But the wool industry continued to thrive.

During the mid-1900s, many more indigenous people were sent to remote stations, away from their traditional lands, or moved into towns after camps and reserves were closed. But in later years, the government began returning the remaining reserves and housing settlements to indigenous ownership and control.

In the 1990s, Native Title gave indigenous people the right to claim land access along the Darling River, and today the MurrayDarling basin has many areas where people can rediscover indigenous heritage, including Gundabooka, Kinchega, Mungo, Mutawintji, Paroo-Darling and Sturt National Parks.

Clancy of
the Overflow

A. B. (Banjo) Paterson

I had written him a letter which I had, for
    want of better
Knowledge, sent to where I met him down
    the Lachlan, years ago.
He was shearing when I knew him, so I sent
    the letter to him,
Just 'on spec' addressed as follows: 'Clancy of
    The Overflow'.

And an answer came directed in a writing
    unexpected,
(and I think the same was written with a
    thumbnail dipped in tar).

'Twas his shearing mate who wrote it, and
  verbatim I will quote it:
'Clancy's gone to Queensland droving, and
  we don't know where he are.'

In my wild erratic fancy, visions came to
  me of Clancy
Gone a-droving 'down the Cooper' where
  the western drovers go.
As the stock are slowly stringing, Clancy
  rides behind them singing,
For the drover's life has pleasures that the
  townfolk never know.

And the bush has friends to meet him, and
  their kindly voices greet him
In the murmur of the breezes and the river
  on its bars,
And he sees the vision splendid of the
  sunlit plains extended,
And at night the wondrous glory of the
  everlasting stars.

I am sitting in my dingy little office, where
   a stingy
Ray of sunlight struggles feebly down
   between the houses tall,
And the foetid air and gritty of the dusty,
   dirty city
Through the open window floating, spreads
   it's foulness over all.

And in place of lowing cattle, I can hear the
   fiendish rattle
Of the tramways and the buses making
   hurry down the street,
And the language uninviting of the gutter
   children fighting,
Comes fitfully and faintly through the
   ceaseless tramp of feet.

And the hurrying people daunt me, and
    their pallid faces haunt me
As they shoulder one another in their rush
    and nervous haste,
With their eager eyes and greedy, and their
    stunted forms and weedy,
For townsfolk have no time to grow, they
    have no time to waste.

And I somehow rather fancy that I'd like to
    trade with Clancy,
Like to take a turn at droving where the
    seasons come and go,
While he faced the round eternal of the
    cashbook and the journal —
But I doubt he'd suit the office, Clancy of
    'The Overflow'.

Other Titles

in the Clancy of
the Outback Series

Chookshed Blues

Roadkill Rescue

Shearing Time